For Misty, Zooey, Shah, Bambi, Beaumont, Lila, and all the kittens. —J.S.
For Ron and Grace. —L.W.

Text ©1998 by Joan Sweeney. Illustrations ©1998 by Leslie Wu.
All rights reserved.

On the gatefold: *The Rehearsal on the Stage*
The Metropolitan Museum of Art, Bequest of Mrs. H. O. Havemeyer, 1929.
The H.O. Havemeyer Collection (29.100.39)
Photograph © 1978 The Metropolitan Museum of Art

Art direction by Lucy Nielsen and Madeleine Budnick.
Book design by Lucy Nielsen. Typeset in Berling and Dorchester Script.
The illustrations in this book were rendered in pastels.
Printed in Hong Kong.

Library of Congress Cataloging-in-Publication Data
Sweeney, Joan, 1930-
Bijou, Bonbon, and Beau : the kittens who danced for Degas /
Joan Sweeney ; illustrated by Leslie Wu.
p. cm
Summary: Three little kittens create a sensation when they join the dancers on-stage of
a Parisian theater known for its ballet and for the artist who paints there.
ISBN 0-8118-1975-2
[1. Cats—Fiction. 2. Ballet dancing—Fiction.
3. Degas, Edgar, 1834-1917—Fiction. 4. Artists—Fiction.]
I. Wu. Leslie, ill. II. Title.
PZ7.S97426Bi   1998   [E]—dc21   97-22571
CIP   AC

Distributed in Canada by Raincoast Books
8680 Cambie Street, Vancouver, British Columbia V6P 6M9

10 9 8 7 6 5 4 3 2 1

Chronicle Books
85 Second Street, San Francisco, California 94105

Web Site: www.chronbooks.com

Bijou, Bonbon & Beau

The Kittens Who Danced for Degas

by Joan Sweeney

illustrated by Leslie Wu

chronicle books · san francisco

*O*n a blustery day long ago, a weary cat crossed a bridge over the river Seine in Paris. All afternoon, she had been searching for a warm place.

When she thought she could go no further, she came to a theater where ballet was performed. The theater was known throughout Paris. A talented artist often came there to sketch.

No one saw the cat slip through the back door. The next morning, the wardrobe mistress discovered the cat—now a mama with three tiny kittens.

"What angels!" Madame Duvay exclaimed. She lined a basket with some soft leotards for their home.

The ballerinas were enchanted. They named the mama cat Marmalade for her orange stripes. And they called her babies Bijou, Bonbon and Beau.

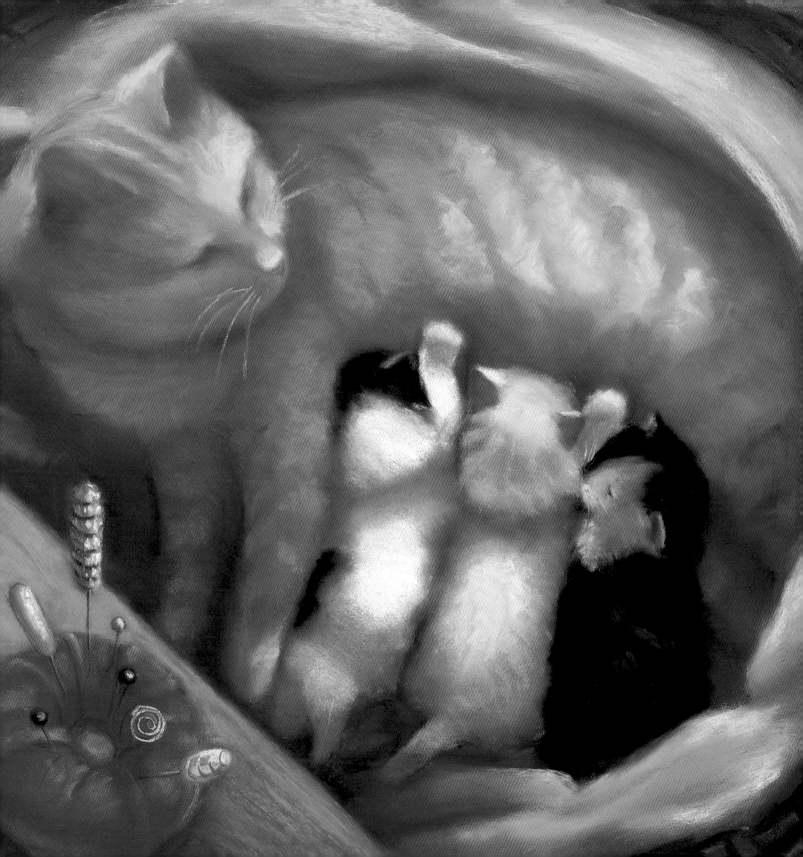

$\mathcal{E}$ach day before rehearsal, the dancers, stagehands and musicians all stopped by to visit. The artist often came too.

"Hush," Madame Duvay would scold when their chatter grew too loud. "You are making Marmalade nervous."

One day while the ballerinas were practicing, Marmalade decided to move her kittens to a quieter spot. She was just carrying the last kitten off when a frightful voice boomed:

"*Sacre bleu!*" It was Armand Klenk, the stage manager. No one was safe from his temper.

Flustered, Madame Duvay dropped her pincushion. Meanwhile, Marmalade escaped with the kittens, but not before Klenk roared, "Get rid of those animals at once!"

From one of the empty seats in front of the theater came a softer voice. "Calm down, Klenk. They'll keep the mice away." It was the artist, quietly sketching.

"Very well," huffed Klenk. He knew the artist's drawings helped sell tickets. "But keep those creatures out of my sight," he growled to Madame Duvay.

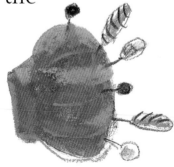

From then on, Madame Duvay did her best to hide Bijou, Bonbon and Beau. But before long, they grew too big for their basket. And their curiosity grew just as fast.

Oh, the mischief they got into! They chased after the ballerinas and slept in their toeshoes. They got tangled in Madame Duvay's thread and ran off with her ribbons.

Still, no one could resist them. Not the gruff stage-hands. Not the old violinist who played at rehearsals. Not the stern balletmaster who tried to hide his smile. And not the artist who sketched the dancers—not even when the kittens jumped on his sketchbook, leaving tiny paw prints in his precise strokes of pastel.

By then the troupe was practicing long and hard. They were going to perform a new ballet, and everything had to be perfect.

Madame Duvay was busy with her needle and thread. She had no time to think about kittens. Every tutu had to fit just right.

At last, opening night arrived. Every seat in the theater was taken. When the curtain went up, the ballerinas never looked lovelier. And they never performed so well. Their jetés were flawless, their pirouettes perfect.

*A*ll at once, lured by the whirling feet, the kittens charged from the wings. They pounced on the dancers' ankles and spun in front of the footlights. They crouched low, then sprang through the air. The ballerinas could barely stay on their toes.

Over the music came the sound of soft chuckles. The artist, watching from the wings, chuckled too. Before long, laughter filled the entire theater.

Quickly, Klenk brought the curtain down. Gritting his teeth, he announced a brief intermission. Backstage, he searched for the kittens. "Find them!" he raged to one and all. "And then, *out they go!*"

Madame Duvay was nearly in tears. The poor kittens! They did not deserve the cold streets.

The next day, however, the ballet was the talk of the town.
Suddenly, everyone wanted tickets. All of Paris wanted to see
the kittens who danced.

What could Klenk say? A full theater was all he could
ask for. The kittens were allowed to stay. Never again did they
stop a performance—Madame Duvay made certain of that.
But for the rest of the season, when the ballerinas took their
final bows, they held Marmalade and her family in their arms.

"Bravo, Marmalade! Bravo, Bijou, Bonbon and Beau!"

Today, all the world loves Degas's
images of the ballet—like this one, called
The Rehearsal on the Stage.
And the story about Bijou, Bonbon
and Beau—did it really happen?
Turn the page, and look very closely.
Down among the shadows, it's possible
you may see their tiny paw prints.

Ballet was a favorite source of inspiration for the French artist Edgar Degas (1834–1917).

While many considered him an Impressionist, Degas disliked painting nature and preferred to work indoors. He chose lively, theatrical subjects and unique composition. His studies of ballerinas are known for their mastery of motion and for reviving the lost art of pastel.

Later in life, when his eyesight began to fail, Degas created some of his finest ballet studies using dramatic lines and vibrant color. As a painter, pastelist, and sculptor, Degas is considered one of the great artists of his time.

Edgar Degas, *The Rehearsal on the Stage*
Pastel over brush-and-ink drawing on paper, 21" x 28½"